TO MY FAMILY: PAT, JAKE, CARLY, MOM AND DAD

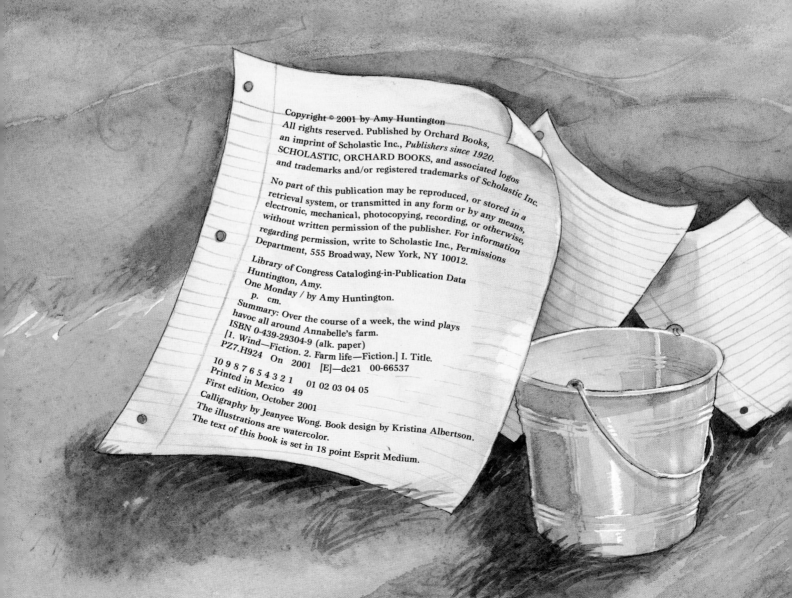

Library of Congress Cataloging-in-Publication Data
Huntington, Amy.
One Monday / by Amy Huntington.
  p.   cm.
Summary: Over the course of a week, the wind plays
havoc all around Annabelle's farm.
ISBN 0-439-29304-9 (alk. paper)
[1. Wind—Fiction. 2. Farm life—Fiction.] I. Title.
PZ7.H924  On  2001  [E]—dc21  00-66537

10 9 8 7 6 5 4 3 2 1    01 02 03 04 05
Printed in Mexico  49
First edition, October 2001
Calligraphy by Jeanyee Wong. Book design by Kristina Albertson.
The illustrations are watercolor.
The text of this book is set in 18 point Esprit Medium.

# One Monday

## by Amy Huntington

Orchard Books / New York

An Imprint of Scholastic Inc.

One Monday on Annabelle's farm, it was so windy, the tin roof banged like thunder.

By afternoon the pigs' curly tails were straightened out like rulers.

On Tuesday morning it was so windy,
all the hens' feathers turned inside out,

and Annabelle almost did too!

On Wednesday it was so windy, carrots and turnips twisted out of the garden beds, and the corn picked itself.

By Thursday it was so windy,
sunflower heads spun off like flying saucers,
and one poor blue jay went for a dizzy ride.

By the time Friday rolled around, it was so windy,
frogs belly-surfed on the waves in the trough,

and the cow had lost most of her spots.

WHSSSH

On Saturday it was so windy, cats began to whoosh across the barnyard.

Even Annabelle had trouble
keeping her feet on the ground.

Finally, on Sunday, after a long week,
the wind blew so hard, it simply blew itself
right out of town.

The next day, Monday, it rained so hard . . .